For Sheila,
the best mum in the world. A.S.

To Richard, Phoebe, Max and Molly,
the best family in the world. C.H.

OXFORD
UNIVERSITY PRESS

Great Clarendon Street, Oxford OX2 6DP

Oxford University Press is a department of the University of Oxford.
It furthers the University's objective of excellence in research, scholarship,
and education by publishing worldwide in

Oxford   New York

Athens Auckland Bangkok Bogotá Buenos Aires Calcutta
Cape Town Chennai Dar es Salaam Delhi Florence Hong Kong Istanbul
Karachi Kuala Lumpur Madrid Melbourne Mexico City Mumbai
Nairobi Paris São Paulo Shanghai Singapore Taipei Tokyo Toronto Warsaw

and associated companies in Berlin Ibadan

ISBN 0 19 279039 0 (hardback)
ISBN 0 19 272378 2 (paperback)

1 3 5 7 9 10 8 6 4 2

Printed in Malaysia

The Truth About Families

Andrea Shavick

Illustrated by Charlotte Hard

OXFORD

UNIVERSITY PRESS

Families

You can't choose your mum or your dad or your brothers or your sisters or your grandparents or your uncles or your aunties or your cousins.

You just have to learn to live with what you've got.

Brothers and sisters

Brothers and sisters can be difficult to live with because they are so annoying.

If they're younger than you, they always want to play with your things.

If they're older than you, they never let you play with their things. It's not fair.

But when your mum or dad gets cross it can be very useful having someone to blame.

Parents

Mums and dads can also be difficult to live with because they're always telling you what to do.

Of course, they never do any of those things themselves!

And they're so embarrassing.

They say things they're not supposed to.
They do things you wish they wouldn't.

And the more friends you're with,
the more embarrassing they are.

Uncles and aunts

Slightly easier to get along with are uncles and aunts. Because they're your parents' brothers or sisters, they're always on your side.

They have you to stay for the weekend.

They take you out to
posh restaurants,

and buy you things
your parents won't.

They even take you to pop concerts.

Grandparents

Then there are your grandparents. Your parents' parents. Also quite easy to get along with. They always think you're gorgeous.

And with memories like elephants, they can remember right back to when they were as little as you.

Funny thing is, they never remember
what time to put you to bed.

Or that you're not allowed that many sweets.
Quite lucky really.

Big or small

But does the size of your family make any difference as to how well you get on with them?

Small families can be quite cosy, but that doesn't mean they never have arguments.

Large families just give you more choice
about who to argue with next!
Some people have step-mums and dads,
step-brothers and sisters as well ...

Ben's step-grandma
(his grandad's 2nd wife)

Ben's grandad

Ben's Aunt   Ben's Uncle Dan

Ben's great-grandma
and grandad

Ben's baby
cousin Phoebe

Ben's mum

Ben's dad

Ben

Ben's brother and sister

...which can
be really
confusing.

Big families

If you've got a really big family, how about making name badges for them all?

At least everyone will know who they're arguing with.

Whatever your family is like, one thing is certain. Every single person is completely different from everyone else.

When you go out

And because they are all different, that's where the fun really begins.

For instance, when your family has to go out somewhere, is everyone ready to go at the same time?
No, of course not.
That would be far too sensible.

Once you get where you're going, does everyone
want to stay together and do the same thing?
You guessed it . . .

Mess

And look at the amount of mess each one of them makes. There's bound to be someone in your family who is incredibly tidy.

And another one who thinks 'tidy' means just being able to see the floor.

My room

Mum and Dad's room

And the people who nag you to tidy up the most, are often the ones who never throw anything away.

Alex's room

Emma's room

Staying at home

At least when you stay at home everybody in your family gets a chance to do what they want.

Like playing football, or lying underneath the car, or knocking down bits of the house, or fighting.

Fighting and rowing

Yes, fighting. Because all parents scream and shout and nag their children.

Turn it off!

Go and tidy your room now!

Put on a clean jumper, young lady.

I'm counting to three ...starting now!

No TV until you've done your homework.

He started it!

I don't care who started it!

Sometimes they scream and shout at each other as well.

Oh no it's not, it's that way.

I've got the map, it's this way!

And in every family, brothers and sisters argue with each other. But it's all right. You're supposed to fight with your brother or sister.

Families can be fun!

Sometimes getting on with your family
can be very hard work. But doing
things together can also be fun.
The truth about families is that
you can't choose them.

But the other truth about families
is that you probably wouldn't want to
choose anyone else's.